Mystery Cat and the Monkey Business

by Susan Saunders
Illustrated by Eileen Christelow

A Bantam Skylark Book
Toronto • New York • London • Sydney • Auckland

RL4, 008–011

MYSTERY CAT AND THE MONKEY BUSINESS
A Bantam Skylark Book / November 1986

Skylark Books is a registered trademark of Bantam Books, Inc.
Registered in U.S. Patent and Trademark Office and elsewhere.
Mystery Cat is a trademark of Cloverdale Press Inc.
Produced by Cloverdale Press Inc.

ISBN 0-553-15452-4

Published simultaneously in the United States and Canada

PRINTED IN THE UNITED STATES OF AMERICA

C w   0 9 8 7 6 5 4 3 2

Chapter One

"The circus is here!" Andrew McCoy shouted as he ran into the house. His red hair was standing up every which way.

"The circus is here!" his brown-haired twin, Michael, echoed, following close on his brother's heels.

"What circus?" demanded Hillary Barnett. She was keeping her best friend, Kelly Ann McCoy, company. Kelly Ann was baby-sitting her seven-year-old brothers for a few hours after school.

"The Baker Family Circus," Kelly Ann replied. "It'll be in the empty lot at the end of Garland Park for eight days, until September twenty-third. I saw a poster in the window of the Superette."

"We just talked to Billy Johnson," declared Andrew. "He said that he and his dad drove past the park a few minutes ago. The big tent was all spread out on the ground."

"They're going to raise it with elephants!" Michael added. "Can we go see?"

"Let's do!" Hillary said, putting down the

magazine she and Kelly Ann had been looking at. "I love elephants."

"Okay," Kelly Ann agreed. "I'll leave a message for Mom in case she gets back before we do." She hopped up and wrote a few lines on a small blackboard next to the refrigerator.

"Hurry!" Andrew urged. "I want to see the tent go up!"

"That should do it," Kelly Ann said. As they rushed out the front door, they were stopped short by a loud yowl. On the steps stood a scruffy gray cat. He was big and lanky, with old battle scars all over his body. He had a notched left ear and a kink in his tail.

"M.C.!" Hillary exclaimed. "It's too early for dinner." She reached down to pet the tomcat, but he yowled again and turned his back on her.

"He *does* sound hungry," Kelly Ann said. "Wait a sec. I'll give him a snack."

Ignoring her brothers' impatient groans, Kelly Ann dashed back into the house. She reappeared a few moments later with a blue plastic bowl full of Cat Crunchies. "This should tide you over, M.C.," she said, setting it down in front of him.

"Now can we go?" Andrew prodded.

"Come on!" Michael added.

"Okay," Kelly Ann said, giving the cat a final pat. Then they all set off for the park, the twins in the lead.

2

As they rounded the corner, the girls looked back, half-expecting M.C. to be following them. But he seemed much more interested in his Cat Crunchies than in their departure.

"I can't believe you ever thought Lancelot was a good name for M.C.," Hillary said. "It's much too mushy for a tough-looking guy like him."

"Mushy! Lancelot was King Arthur's bravest, most noble knight!" replied Kelly Ann. "I can't believe you ever thought *Frank* was a good name for him. It's much too plain for a cat who's had so many exciting adventures."

"Yeah, but Frank was just short for frankfurter. Don't forget he was busy stealing some from my mom's grocery bag the first time I saw him," Hillary reminded her.

Kelly Ann had to laugh. "That cat! He's always hungry! I guess it's from all those years of not knowing where his next meal was coming from. But even now, with both you and me feeding him, he never seems to get enough."

Hillary grinned at her friend. "I guess it's a good thing those police officers told us they'd already named him Mystery Cat. We might have ended up calling him B.P. instead of M.C."

"B.P.?" Kelly Ann looked puzzled.

"Short for Bottomless Pit," Hillary replied. "Let's see... 'Here, B.P. Here, kitty, kitty.'" She shook her head. "Nah, it never would have stuck. It sounds too much like a car horn. You know—*beepie, beepie.*"

Kelly Ann poked her friend in the ribs. "Besides that, there's a good reason those officers named him Mystery Cat, as you very well know."

The girls walked on in silence for a moment. Kelly Ann remembered that day in the police station when they'd first met. About two weeks before that, each of them had found—and named—a scruffy stray tomcat with a notch in his ear and a kink in his tail. And each of them had adopted him against her parents' wishes.

When Kelly Ann's mother protested that the McCoys couldn't afford to feed another mouth, Kelly Ann had pleaded with her. "But, Mom, I'm sure he'd eat table scraps. Or I could use some of my baby-sitting money to buy cat food." And so at last Mrs. McCoy was won over. Though "Lancelot" was never allowed in the house, Kelly Ann was permitted to fix up a bed for him in the garage.

Meanwhile, on the other side of town, Hillary Barnett had pestered her parents, whom she called by their first names—Glynis and George—into letting her keep "Frank."

"But he's bound to have fleas and goodness knows what else," Glynis had said. "Speak to your father when he gets home." But, of course, Hillary's father let her keep the cat.

4

Then by chance, a week or so later, both eleven-year-old girls had ended up at the police station. One reported her cat missing, and one reported her missing cat returned. That was when they'd first met. And that was when they'd discovered that the big gray cat was leading a double life.

He would arrive at Kelly Ann's house after she got home from Windsor Middle School. He would stay for dinner and take an early-evening nap. Then, after a midnight prowl, he'd turn up at Hillary's house to spend the rest of the night on a feather pillow in her bedroom. In the morning, he'd have breakfast and hang around until the school car picked her up for Lincoln Country Day School. At the McCoys' he ate regular cat food and seemed to enjoy it. At the Barnetts' he dined on the leftovers of Glynis and George's gourmet cooking and always meowed for seconds.

But no sooner had the girls sorted all this out than they'd discovered that the cat had yet another identity.

"From your description, that sounds like old Mystery Cat," a police officer had told them. "We call him that because he seems to have a sixth sense for trouble. He turns up at every traffic jam, fire, and arrest."

"And if it *is* M.C.," his partner added, "you may as well share him, because *nobody* will ever own that cat."

From that moment on, the girls had shared the cat—renamed M.C. And they'd shared a close friendship as well.

"Remember when we first met?" Kelly Ann looked at her friend fondly. "I thought you were nothing but a snobby private-school rich kid."

Hillary snorted. "And I thought you were a cat-napper!" She shook her head. "Who would have thought we'd end up best friends?"

"Or that M.C. really would live up to his name and get us involved in mysteries," Kelly Ann added. "So far he's helped us stop a couple of counterfeiters. He also helped us catch the guy who was stealing all those purebred cats. I wonder what will be next."

"Maybe nothing," Hillary said in a disgusted way. "These days, the only thing he wants to investigate is his food dish! All he ever does is eat and sleep. He's never where the action is anymore.

She should have known better.

Chapter Two

"Look!" Michael said. "M.C.'s coming to the circus, too."

Just as Kelly Ann, Hillary, and the twins reached Garland Park, the big gray cat suddenly jumped out of a clump of bayberry bushes. He trotted up the path in front of them, his crooked tail high in the air, as if he were leading the way.

"Think we should take him home?" Kelly Ann asked. "There's going to be a lot happening —he could get hurt."

"He'd only follow us again," Hillary told her. "You know how stubborn he is."

"If we run, maybe he won't be able to keep up with us," Andrew suggested, breaking into a trot. But M.C. easily kept pace. So in the end they gave in and let him come along.

"There it is!" Michael shouted when they reached the end of the park.

A huge, round tent was spread across the vacant lot. Side poles held the edges of the tent off the ground, so that it looked like a big red-and-white-striped bowl. Out of the middle of the bowl, a center pole soared high into the air.

A flag snapped in the breeze from its tip.

"Look! Elephants!" Andrew said breathlessly.

Around the tent tramped two elephants wearing shiny leather harnesses. They swayed majestically across the lot, flapping their ears and testing the air with their trunks.

As the children joined a small crowd of people, a man hooked thick ropes to the elephants' harnesses. Then the giant animals pulled thousands of pounds of heavy canvas straight up the center pole.

"Ah!" the crowd exclaimed. The red-and-white-striped bowl had been transformed into a circus tent!

With the help of the elephants, workmen raised the quarter poles, which stood halfway between the center and the outside edges of the tent. Carefully they placed them into sockets in the canvas. Then the side wall was attached. It hung like a curtain from the top of the side poles to the ground. The tent was complete! The elephants disappeared behind it.

"Let's go see where the elephants live," Hillary suggested.

"Yes!" the twins chorused.

"All right, but no running off," Kelly Ann said. "And I'm *carrying* M.C."

M.C. had never really liked being held. But there was so much to see and smell that he forgot

9

to squirm when Kelly Ann scooped him up.

Smaller tents had already been raised at the front of the main tent. In one of them, men were setting up cotton candy machines and popcorn poppers.

Hillary peeped through the door of another tent. Inside were a camel, three llamas, and a tiny cream-colored horse. "Isn't it cute?" she said.

"No elephants," Michael said, disappointed.

"Maybe they're over by those four big red trucks," Hillary suggested.

They walked around the main tent into a jumble of vans and cars and campers. The four tractor-trailers were painted the same deep red as the stripes in the circus tent. They were decorated with the words BAKER FAMILY CIRCUS, in fancy gold letters three feet high.

Beyond the first truck were the elephants—not just two, but a whole row of them. "Wow!" Andrew said. "Five grown-ups and four babies!"

"And do they eat!" a voice said from behind them. They turned to see a thin, wiry man with a big gray moustache and an armful of hay. "It comes to about one hundred thousand pounds of hay a year for the grown ones," the man went on. "They like bread, too, and fruit and vegetables." He smiled at them. "I'm Al the elephant man, by the way. Want to help me feed them?"

"Can we?" Andrew asked Kelly Ann.

"We'll be careful," Michael said.

"I'll keep an eye on them," Al promised the girls. He handed an armload of hay to Andrew and another to Michael. Then he grabbed some more for himself and led the twins over to the elephants.

"Dump it on the ground in front of them. He won't hurt you," Al said to Andrew, who had backed away as a trunk reached toward him. "That's Hector. He wants to see who you are."

The tip of Hector's trunk slid gently up Andrew's arm. It came to a rest for a second on the boy's bright red hair. Andrew giggled. "That tickles!" he said. Then Hector grabbed some hay with his trunk and stuffed it into his mouth.

The two girls sat down on a big overturned tub to watch. Kelly Ann kept a tight grip on M.C. The gray cat's ears were pointed straight forward. They quivered as he took in the new sights and sounds.

In an open space next to a small silver trailer, two women in blue leotards practiced double backflips on a trampoline. Nearby a plump man was putting some poodles through their paces. They rolled over, walked on their hind legs, and even turned somersaults.

Then the door of the silver trailer opened, and an older woman stepped out. She was taking a sleek black panther for a walk! It wore a

11

rhinestone collar, and its bright eyes gleamed in its dark face.

"Don't you think M.C. would look like that if he were ten times bigger?" Kelly Ann asked.

The panther yawned, showing enormous white teeth and a bright pink tongue.

"Well..." Hillary answered, "at least the *yawn* is the same."

Both girls giggled.

"You know it's nice back here," Kelly Ann said, sighing contentedly.

Hillary nodded. "Kind of homey and peaceful and—" She was interrupted by a loud crash and an angry shout.

Suddenly a dark, fuzzy monkey, not even two feet tall, hurtled through the back door of the third trailer truck. It was followed closely by two large men wearing overalls. One of the men was waving a length of pipe!

The monkey zigzagged among the cars and trailers and people. As Kelly Ann and Hillary stood up to see better, the monkey whizzed right by them. It grabbed M.C.'s dangling tail and gave it a good yank as it scooted past!

"*Mrow!*" M.C. screeched. Hissing and clawing, he struggled out of Kelly Ann's arms. The gray cat had joined the chase!

"Catch him!" Kelly Ann shrieked.

She and Hillary raced after the monkey, M.C., and the two men in overalls, in that order.

But they didn't have far to run. The chase ended when the monkey scrambled up a red-and-white-striped pole. And there it sat, making rude faces and chattering loudly at the small but angry crowd gathering below.

Hillary grabbed M.C., who was still raging and showed every sign of wanting to join the monkey on the pole. Now that it was sitting still, Hillary could see that the monkey wasn't much bigger than M.C. Its thick coat was short and wiry, and so dark it looked almost black.

The door of a nearby camper opened, and a young woman stuck her head out. "Problems?" she asked. Her eyebrows were jet-black, but her hair was whitish blond. She also had very red lips, and—as Hillary said later—"the longest nails in the world," painted to match.

"Pico hasn't been naughty again, has he?" the woman asked with a playful look.

"Naughty?" the man holding the pipe roared. "Naughty! The little creep was messing up my stuff!"

"Zack!" the woman called over her shoulder. Then she disappeared inside the camper and closed the door. The girls could hear the murmur of voices.

The door opened again, and a man with short black hair stepped out. His eyes looked puffy with sleep.

"Jennings," the man with the pipe said, "the

next time I catch that monkey of yours in the sleeper. . .you'd better start working on another act!" He thumped the camper with the pipe.

"Because half of yours will be gone!" the second man added, staring straight at the monkey in case Zack had missed the point.

The dark-haired man shook his head in wonder. "I can't believe two grown men can get so upset by one little ol' monkey," he said. "It's no big deal. Pico's just naturally curious."

"Curiosity killed the cat!" the second man snapped.

Hillary hugged M.C. tighter.

"Just keep that monkey away from us!" the first man warned Zack again. Then he and his friend spun around and stalked off.

Zack reached up and pulled Pico off the pole. Then he caught sight of Hillary and Kelly Ann and scowled. "You kids aren't supposed to be back here," he snarled. "You want to look at the animals, you pay to see the show." Clutching the monkey by the scruff of its neck, he stepped back into the camper and slammed the door.

"I guess we'd better leave," Kelly Ann said to Hillary in a low voice. Then she looked anxiously around. "Oh, no!" she exclaimed. "Where are the twins? I was so worried about M.C. I forgot all about them!"

"Right here, miss." It was Al the elephant man, with Andrew and Michael in tow. "Don't

15

pay any attention to Zack Jennings," he said. "If you're with me, it's okay."

"Well, we'd better be getting home anyway," Kelly Ann said. "Mom is going to start wondering what's keeping us."

"Thanks, Mr. Al..." Andrew began.

"...For letting us feed the elephants and everything!" Michael finished.

"Come back anytime; we'll be right here for eight days," Al told them. "See the show, too."

"We will," the children promised.

They walked around the big tent, M.C. squirming to be put down. "No you don't!" Hillary told him. I know you—you'd be after that monkey in a flash!"

In the end she carried the protesting cat all the way to the McCoys', just to make sure he didn't try anything sneaky. And when she finally put him down on the back porch, he walked stiffly across the yard with such an offended look on his face that the girls burst out laughing.

M.C. worked off a little steam by bullying the McCoys' dog, Samantha, out of her doghouse. Then he sat down in it and began to wash up, as if he didn't have a care in the world.

"Poor Sam," Hillary said, patting the mournful dog. "But at least M.C.'s forgotten about the monkey."

"I wouldn't be too sure about that," Kelly Ann said. "M.C. has a long memory."

16

Chapter Three

The next day was Kelly Ann's first time to baby-sit for the Darbys. It was also the first time she had gotten a job baby-sitting for a family she didn't know well. Mr. McCoy had reshingled the Darbys' house a few weeks before. It was then that he had given Mrs. Darby his daughter's name.

"They're new in Windsor, and she was looking for a good baby-sitter," he reported to Kelly Ann. "I told her we had the best in town."

The Darbys had two children—Sara, who was three, and a brand-new baby, Jonathan. Mrs. Darby had called to ask if Kelly Ann could watch Sara while she took the baby to the doctor for his checkup. "We're number nine, the third house from the corner on Pine Lane," Mrs. Darby told her. "Jonathan's appointment is at two. So I'd like to leave home by one-thirty."

Kelly Ann finished her lunch in a hurry. She changed into a pair of new blue pants and a blue-and-white-striped T-shirt. She wanted to make a good impression. "I should be back around four," she called to her mother on her way out the door.

She decided not to ride her bike. Pine Lane wasn't too far away, and she knew a footpath through the park that would be quicker than sticking to the roads on her bike. She hadn't gone a block when she realized she wasn't alone.

"Mrow!" she heard behind her.

"M.C., where did you come from?" Kelly Ann groaned.

The gray cat looked up at her, his eyes narrowed to slits in the sunlight. He purred smugly.

"M.C., please go home," said Kelly Ann. "Andrew and Michael will play fetch with you. This is business—it's what keeps you in cat food!"

M.C. sat down in Kelly Ann's shadow. He turned and licked his shoulder.

Kelly Ann checked her watch. Ten minutes after one—only twenty more minutes to get there! "I don't have time for this," she said out loud. She picked up M.C. and trotted back to her yard, where she placed him on the front steps.

"Stay!" she said sharply. Then she jogged back up the street. Half a block away she looked back over her shoulder. She was expecting a repeat performance, but M.C. was sitting where she'd left him. He was cleaning himself indignantly, as if trying to smooth down the fur she had ruffled.

Kelly Ann arrived at the Darbys' out of

breath but on time. She recognized the house as soon as she turned the corner. "Shingles by McCoy," she thought proudly.

Mrs. Darby was standing in the driveway next to a red car. A plump woman with a friendly grin, she was trying to hold the baby in one arm. She was using her free hand to make Sara let go of her skirt.

"You're Kelly Ann," Mrs. Darby said with a sigh of relief. "I'm glad you could come. Sara, sweetie, Mommy will be back soon. Please let go of my skirt."

"No!" Sara said firmly.

"Jonathan has to see the doctor," Mrs. Darby told the three-year-old. "You don't want to see the doctor, do you?"

"No!" Sara replied, but she kept her grip on Mrs. Darby's hem.

"Kelly Ann, would you mind holding Jonathan for a minute?" Mrs. Darby handed her the baby. She leaned down to pull Sara's fingers away from her skirt. In response, Sara shrieked as loudly as she could.

"She's just going through a phase," Mrs. Darby told Kelly Ann, taking the baby back. She opened the back door of the car and settled Jonathan into his car seat. Then she slid into the front seat.

"Sorry to rush off," she said over Sara's screams, "but I hate to be late, especially on a

Saturday—the office is so crowded. I've left the doctor's number for you on the kitchen table if there's any problem. And don't worry—Sara will stop yelling as soon as I've left." She waited while a large white truck marked MAPLE LEAF COMMUNICATIONS went by. Then she backed down the drive into the street.

As the car disappeared, Sara's shrieks faded into whines and then sniffs. She pushed her hair out of her face and looked up at Kelly Ann. "What's that sound?" she asked.

Kelly Ann listened. "It's a band," she answered. "The band at the circus."

"I want to play circus," Sara said.

"All right," Kelly Ann agreed. Anything to keep Sara from screaming again.

"I'm the lion tamer—you be the lion," Sara directed. "You have to roar."

"*Rrrrra!*" Kelly Ann roared.

"More!" said Sara.

"*Rrrrrow!*" Kelly Ann roared louder.

"There's a real lion," Sara said suddenly, pointing behind Kelly Ann.

Kelly Ann spun around. The "lion" at her feet was gray, with a notched ear and a kink in his tail.

"Not again!" she exclaimed. "M.C., why don't you stay at home?"

"I want to play with the lion!" Sara said. She made a grab for M.C. that just missed his ears.

The cat backed off and hissed a warning.

"I think we'll go inside for a while." Kelly Ann picked Sara up and started for the house. "M.C.— The lion isn't used to small children."

Sara drew in her breath for a scream. But Kelly Ann headed her off: "Don't you want to show me your toys?"

Sara let out her breath in a rush. "Okay," she agreed.

The Darby's home was a square two-story house. Sara's room was in front, at the top of the stairs. It was painted a light green. There were bright posters on the walls and shelves full of toys. Kelly Ann looked out the window at the lawn below, but she couldn't see the cat. "How did he find me?" she wondered. "He's getting to be almost like a bloodhound!"

"Read me this," Sara commanded. She handed Kelly Ann a small book with a yellow cover.

"Please," Kelly Ann prompted.

"Please," Sara said.

" 'A Day at the Circus,' " Kelly Ann began.

As Kelly Ann read, Sara recited the sentences along with her. Obviously, she knew the story by heart. But after a while her attention wandered. She walked over to the window and looked out.

"Oh, look!" she squealed. "There's a monkey!"

Kelly Ann smiled. If M.C. was a lion, the monkey was undoubtedly a squirrel. Sara had quite an imagination. "Mmm-hum," Kelly Ann agreed, barely looking through the window. Sure enough, a squirrel was running along the thick wires that connected a nearby telephone pole to the house.

"Want to play with my blocks?" Sara asked, suddenly changing the subject.

"Sure," said Kelly Ann.

Sara pulled a big cardboard boxful of wooden blocks out of the closet. She and Kelly Ann had just started building a castle when they heard a siren coming up Pine Lane.

"What could that be?" Kelly Ann wondered out loud. She hurried to the window and looked out. A Windsor police car had pulled up to the curb across the street. Two patrolmen climbed out. "Officer Waters and Officer Haney!" said Kelly Ann. She knew several of the Windsor policemen well because of M.C. and his mysteries.

"Police!" Sara said as she saw the men in uniform.

"I'm going to see!" She hurried out of her room and was halfway down the stairs before Kelly Ann caught up with her.

"I don't think that's such a good idea," Kelly Ann said, hanging on to Sara's skirt.

Sara let loose with a high-pitched scream.

"On the other hand," Kelly Ann said, "maybe it'd be all right...if we stay in our own yard."

The scream died down, and a moment later Kelly Ann and Sara walked out onto the lawn.

Number twelve Pine Lane was a two-story house like the Darbys'. The girls saw the patrolmen come around the side of it, accompanied by a gray-haired couple. Both the man and the woman were talking excitedly.

"You can see better from here, officers," the man said loudly. He led the policemen to a tall maple tree at the side of the house. "There he is!" He pointed up into the branches. "There's the thief!"

"And there's my pocketbook, right next to him!" the woman added.

As the patrolmen gazed upward, there was a loud drawn out "Mro-owww" from behind the curtain of leaves.

Kelly Ann would have recognized that voice anywhere. It was M.C.!

Chapter Four

"What's all the excitement across the street?" Hillary screeched her bike to a stop on the sidewalk in front of Kelly Ann and Sara. "Andrew told me where you were," she explained. "I thought I'd stop off on my way home from the orthodontist."

"Who are you?" Sara asked.

"I'm Hillary," Hillary replied. "Who are you?"

"I'm Sara Darby," Sara answered formally. "Want to ride me on your bike?"

"No," Kelly Ann told Sara. Then she turned to her friend. "Hillary, M.C.'s up in that maple tree. I think he's in some kind of trouble."

"You bet he is, if he's in a tree," Hillary said, laying her bike down on the Darbys' lawn. "Once he climbs up, he can *never* get down."

"I think it's more than that," Kelly Ann said, "but I don't want to take Sara over there to find out."

"I'll go," Hillary told her, hurrying across the street. She met Officer Haney on his way to the patrol car.

"I thought you might turn up," Officer Haney said when he saw her.

"M.C.?" Hillary said.

"Right. Up in that tree." He pointed. "The Colwells seem to think that he was involved in a burglary."

"Really?" Hillary said, grinning. "Did he catch the guy?"

"Not the way they tell it," Officer Haney said. "They walked down the street to visit a neighbor. And when they came back they discovered that Mrs. Colwell's pocketbook had been stolen out of her bedroom, along with a watch and some earrings."

"What does M.C. have to do with that?" Hillary asked him.

"Mrs. Colwell heard a noise outside the window. She looked out, and there was M.C. with the pocketbook stuck on a branch next to him," Officer Haney answered. "They're both still up there."

"How is M.C. supposed to have gotten the pocketbook onto the branch?" Hillary protested. "That's crazy!"

Patrolman Haney shrugged and smiled. "That cat turns up in the oddest places," he said.

"He probably just followed Kelly Ann. She's baby-sitting at the house across the street," Hillary told him.

"I'd like to talk to her. Maybe she saw something," Officer Haney said.

"What about M.C.?" Hillary asked. Up in the tree the cat was still yowling.

"I was about to radio for the fire department," Officer Haney told her. "They'll have to send the ladder truck." He reached into the police car and spoke on the radio for a minute. Then he turned to Hillary. "They'll be here soon," he assured her. "In the meantime, I'll talk to Kelly Ann."

But Kelly Ann had very little to tell him. "I got here around one-thirty, then Mrs. Darby left, and Sara and I went up to her room," she said.

"You forgot to tell about the lion," Sara put in.

Officer Haney raised his eyebrows. "The lion?"

"M.C.," Kelly Ann explained. "He showed up just before we went inside."

"And you left him outside?" the policeman asked.

Kelly Ann nodded. "He was in the front yard," she said.

"Did you see where he went?" asked Officer Haney.

"I was reading Sara a story," Kelly Ann answered. "I didn't even look out the window until I heard your siren."

"The monkey. . ." Sara prompted her.

"Monkey?" Hillary repeated, looking

27

puzzled.

"I was reading Sara a circus book," Kelly Ann explained, "and she said she saw a monkey out the window."

"I did!" Sara insisted. "I *did* see a monkey."

"A squirrel," Kelly Ann said in a low voice to the policeman.

Sara looked angry, and she might have started shrieking if Officer Haney hadn't stepped in. "Thank you," he said smiling down at the little girl. "That's a big help."

Sara nodded, satisfied.

Then they heard the rumble of an engine farther down the street.

"A fire truck!" Sara announced, clapping her hands.

The bright yellow truck stopped in front of twelve Pine Lane. After a word with Officer Waters, the driver backed the long truck up the Colwells' driveway until it was parked beneath M.C.'s tree.

Officer Haney crossed the street again to supervise the rescue operation, and Hillary went with him. "So M.C. will know he's got a friend," she told Kelly Ann.

Kelly Ann and Sara watched from the Darbys' as the silver ladder slid up into the maple tree. A fireman climbed up the ladder and disappeared from sight among the leaves. There was a pitiful cry from M.C. "The fireman has pulled

28

him off the branch," Kelly Ann explained to Sara. Then the fireman reappeared, backing down the ladder.

Before he could step down onto the truck, his unwilling companion gave a screech and a growl. The big gray cat clawed his way out of the fireman's grasp and hit the ground with a thud. Hillary tried to catch him, but M.C. hissed and took a swipe at her hand. Then he scooted under a hedge and was gone.

"M.C. was not happy," Hillary said when she rejoined Kelly Ann and Sara.

"We saw," Kelly Ann said. "At least he didn't seem hurt."

Hillary agreed. "A hurt cat isn't going to run like that," she said.

"Look!" Sara ordered. "The fireman is climbing up again."

He was soon back down, this time holding a small dark-green pocketbook. Officer Waters took it from him and opened it so that Mrs. Colwell could look inside. The girls saw her shake her head.

Officer Haney walked back over to the Darbys'. "The purse was empty," he told the girls. "No wallet, no earrings or watch. I guess the burglar took the wallet out, then threw the pocketbook out the second-floor window into the tree to get rid of the evidence. It was just M.C.'s bad luck to be up there."

The girls waited in front until the fire truck left and the police car pulled away.

"What if it wasn't just luck?" Kelly Ann said.

"What do you mean?" asked Hillary.

"Maybe there's a good reason M.C. showed up when he did," Kelly Ann said thoughtfully. "Maybe he's given us a clue to a new mystery."

"Great," Hillary said. "Now all we have to do is figure out what a pocketbook in a tree means."

Chapter Five

On Monday morning, Hillary came in to breakfast to find her father making blueberry waffles. "Where's Glynis?" she asked.

"Still asleep," Mr. Barnett answered. He slipped a waffle onto a plate for Hillary. "She was up late last night working on her speech for the Landmarks Preservation Society."

Hillary sat down at the table. She covered her waffle with maple syrup and took a big bite. "Mmmm!" she complimented her father around a mouthful of waffle.

"Thanks," he responded. "Oh, by the way, there's a picture of a close friend of yours in the paper today."

"A friend of mine?" said Hillary.

Mr. Barnett held out a copy of the *Windsor Watchman*. Hillary's eyes followed her father's finger to a small photo near the bottom of the front page.

"M.C.!" Hillary exclaimed. "That's the picture that was taken when the Windsor Cat Breeders' Association gave him the award for stopping the cat-napper."

M.C. stared defiantly at the camera. Both of his ears pointed forward, his eyes were wide open, and he held his crooked tail stiffly in the air.

"He looks very distinguished," Kelly Ann had remarked at the time. But the article under the picture said nothing about M.C.'s successes as a crime buster!

"*CAT BURGLAR?*" the first paragraph began. It reported the Saturday theft of Mrs. Colwell's wallet and jewelry from an upstairs bedroom of her house. The writer described how M.C. had been found in the tree at the scene of the crime, along with Mrs. Colwell's green pocketbook. Then the article went on to say that two more burglaries had taken place sometime Sunday afternoon. A gold chain and three hundred dollars were stolen from a duplex apartment at Thornton Crescent. A pearl necklace and earrings were taken from another second-floor apartment in the same complex.

Although the doors and first-floor windows of both apartments were wired to burglar alarms, no alarms had been set off. The only lead so far was a muddy cat print on a flagstone terrace—and a description. A neighbor had informed the *Watchman* that he'd seen a gray cat with a crooked tail slinking across the parking lot.

"M.C. never slinks!" Hillary stated firmly.

She smacked the paper down. "George!" she said. "How do we go about suing the *Windsor Watchman?*"

"What for?" Mr. Barnett asked.

"Slander!" Hillary told him. "Or declamation of character, or whatever it's called!"

"Defamation," Mr. Barnett said mildly. "But I'm not sure it applies to animals."

"You mean they can say anything they like about M.C. and get away with it?" Hillary asked, outraged.

Mr. Barnett picked up the paper and looked at the article again. "They haven't really said anything libelous here," he told his daughter. "They've simply reported that M.C. was found in a tree along with Mrs. Colwell's pocketbook." He looked thoughtful. "I wonder what he was doing up there. . . ."

Hillary stuck to the point. "What about 'cat burglar'? Isn't that libelous?"

"The writer was just trying to add a little humor to a rather dull article," said Mr. Barnett.

"Well, I don't think it's a bit funny!" Hillary said. "I think it's—" Then her new private phone rang, and she raced down the hall to her bedroom to answer it.

M.C. was lying on his back on the feather pillow at the end of her bed. When Hillary flung herself down to answer the phone, he opened one sleepy eye in protest.

"Hello?" Hillary said breathlessly.

"Have you seen the paper?" It was Kelly Ann.

"Yes—doesn't it make you mad?" Hillary answered.

"Furious!" Kelly Ann said heatedly. "My dad said there probably wasn't enough news to fill up the issue, or they wouldn't have run such a silly story."

"But they *did* run it," Hillary said. "What about M.C.'s reputation? We've got to make them take it back, Kelly Ann, and the only way to do that is to track down the real thief—quick."

"How?" Kelly Ann asked.

"We'll think of something," Hillary said. "Listen, I have to hang up. It's almost time for the school car, and I haven't given M.C. his breakfast yet. Want to come over this afternoon? We can make a plan of action then."

"Okay," Kelly Ann agreed. "See you later."

Hillary hung up the phone and ran back to the kitchen. Mr. Barnett was putting on his jacket to leave for work in the city. He straightened his tie and gave Hillary a kiss on the top of her head. "Good-bye, sweetie," he said.

"Bye," Hillary answered distractedly. She had opened the refrigerator and was pushing around containers and bowls. Finally she pulled out a platter of smoked salmon, a roast, and some frankfurters. She cut samples of each into small pieces and dumped them onto a dish.

M.C. yawned and stretched when she carried the dish into her bedroom. "Mrow?" he inquired.

"Right—breakfast," Hillary replied. "But *not* in bed." She set the dish on the floor. The gray cat hopped down, tucked his tail neatly around himself, and started to eat.

A horn honked twice outside.

"The car," Hillary muttered. She made sure her window was open far enough for M.C. to get out when he wanted to. Then she stuffed her school books into a backpack and gave M.C. a squeeze. "Do yourself a favor," Hillary called over her shoulder as she dashed to the front door. "Give us a clue we can *use* today, M.C.!"

By the time the car brought Hillary back home from school, Kelly Ann's bike was already leaning against the front steps. Mrs. Griffis, the Barnetts' housekeeper, handed Hillary a tray holding a plate of cookies and two glasses of milk. "Kelly Ann is waiting for you in your room," she said.

Hillary found her friend sitting cross-legged on the floor, staring at the front page of the *Windsor Watchman*.

"The only clues," Kelly Ann said, taking a cookie, "seem to point to a cat—our cat!" She tapped M.C.'s picture with her finger.

"Has M.C. done anything to help us out?" Hillary asked.

Kelly Ann shook her head. "I left him playing hide-and-seek with Andrew and Michael. She sighed. "Maybe it's just as well. At least he'll stay out of the paper."

Hillary picked up the *Watchman* and reread the article. Before she put the paper down, she glanced at the other front-page stories: "Windsor Warriors Kick Off Against Valley Spring Vikings"; "Maple Leaf Communications Improves Cable-TV Services to North Windsor"; "Main Street Merchants Donate New Planters."

"Visiting the scene of the latest crimes might give us some ideas," Kelly Ann said.

"Can't hurt," Hillary said. "Do you know where Thornton Crescent is?"

The Barnetts had moved from the city to Windsor less than a year before. As a result, Hillary didn't know her way around town as well as her friend did.

Kelly Ann nodded. "It's on the north side of the park."

"Let's go!"

The girls scrambled to their feet and hurried outside to get their bikes. "Mrs. Griffis!" Hillary shouted through the kitchen window to the housekeeper. "Please tell Glynis I'm with Kelly Ann. I'll be back by dinner."

"Will do!" Mrs. Griffis called back.

Before long, the girls were speeding up Main Street. "Turn left at the next light," Kelly Ann directed. They rode down a street of older houses and large lawns. "Now right," Kelly Ann said. "There it is, at the end of the block."

The large buildings that made up the Thornton Crescent Apartments looked brand-new. Made of light-colored wood, with slanted roofs and skylights and balconies, they were grouped around an oval swimming pool.

"There sure are lots of apartments," Hillary said. "And there's no one around; the parking lot's almost empty. So how are we ever going to figure out which apartments were burgled? Everyone must still be at work."

"Maybe he can tell us something," Kelly Ann suggested, pointing to a small boy playing on some swings.

"That little kid?" Hillary said doubtfully.

"Don't underestimate little kids," Kelly Ann told her. "Andrew and Michael always know everything that's going on in our neighborhood. I'm going to talk to him."

They left their bikes in the parking lot and walked around the pool. "Hi," Kelly Ann said to the little boy.

Hillary sat down in the swing next to his. "We read about these apartments in the paper," she said.

"Yeah!" The little boy stopped swinging. "A

robber took lots of money and stuff!"

"Do you know which apartments he robbed?" Kelly Ann asked him.

"Sure!" the little boy answered quickly. "Those two at the end of that house." He pointed to the building in the middle. "We were at the circus when it happened, but Mr. Jason saw the cat with the crooked tail."

"M.C.!" Hillary murmured to Kelly Ann.

"Where does Mr. Jason live?" Kelly Ann asked.

"Over there," the little boy said. "The apartment with the blue door."

"Timmy, time to come in," a woman's voice called.

"Coming!" the little boy shouted back. "Bye," he said to the girls.

"Let's talk to Mr. Jason," Kelly Ann suggested. But there was no one home behind the blue door, so the girls took a closer look at the two apartments that had been robbed. Both had sliding glass doors in front, opening onto stone terraces. Both had back doors leading to the parking lot. Each had a small balcony on the second floor, overlooking the pool. But the balconies were much too high to reach from the ground. The apartment on the end had a trellis on its outside wall. "See that small window on the second floor, just above the top of the trellis? What if somebody climbed up and—"

"Hmmm," Kelly Ann said thoughtfully.

"No way," Hillary told her. "That trellis wouldn't support more than fifteen pounds."

"Then how else did that guy get in?" Kelly Ann asked.

Hillary shook her head. "I don't know, but even M.C. is too heavy for that trellis."

The girls walked back to their bikes, feeling discouraged.

"Want to take another look at the Colwells' house?" Kelly Ann said at last. "It's not far."

"Why not?" Hillary answered. "We don't have any other leads."

As they rode away from the Thornton Crescent Apartments, they passed a large, white truck with a cherry picker. It was being used to lift a man in green coveralls to the top of a utility pole. MAPLE LEAF COMMUNICATIONS was written on the truck's door in green script.

"That's the company the *Watchman* article was about," Hillary remarked.

"Yeah. They're stringing the new cable-TV wires. There's a truck on almost every block around here," Kelly Ann said, not sounding interested. "I saw one when I baby-sat for Sara."

Suddenly Hillary motioned Kelly Ann off the road.

"What is it?" Kelly Ann asked her.

"Look!" Hillary said in a breathless whisper. "There's something going on over there."

40

Chapter Six

Kelly Ann looked up and down the quiet street. "Where?" she said doubtfully. "I don't see anything funny going on."

"Get out of sight!" Hillary hissed, pulling her bike into a big green hedge. "Now look up that driveway!"

Kelly Ann peeked through the hedge at a large brick house. A white truck like the one they'd just passed was slowly backing up the driveway. "So?" she said.

"Don't you remember the cat-napper's truck?" Hillary said impatiently. "No one paid any attention to it because it looked like an ice-cream wagon. It was the perfect disguise—and so is this! Who's going to notice one more white truck around here?"

Kelly Ann took a harder look at the truck in the driveway. "The cat-napper's truck was a junky old thing he'd slapped some white paint on," she said. "This truck is very fancy, and it's full of expensive equipment. Nobody would go to so much trouble just to steal a few necklaces and some earrings. Besides, it's got the same

41

sign on the door as all the other trucks around here."

"Then the burglar works for Maple Leaf Communications," Hillary suggested. "That has to be it! Otherwise, what's he doing? None of the other drivers is backing up anyone's driveway—they're all stringing cable from utility poles!"

"That's true," Kelly Ann had to admit.

"It also explains how the burglar got into the duplexes and the Colwells'. He just backed up under an upstairs window, raised that crane, and slipped in and out. If anyone saw him, he could always claim to be wiring for cable and say he got the wrong house."

Kelly Ann still wasn't convinced.

"It's stopping, right under an upstairs window!" Hillary exclaimed. The white truck parked next to the brick house. Several trees screened it from the street, but from their hiding place the girls could see clearly.

"Look. There are two of them," said Kelly Ann. A man wearing a blue shirt and dungarees had suddenly appeared from behind the house.

"He was probably casing the joint!" Hillary told her.

The man in the blue shirt pulled himself up onto the bed of the truck. Then he stepped into the metal basket of the cherry picker and motioned upward with his arms.

The driver leaned forward, a motor started

grinding, and the crane unfolded. It lifted the man in the metal basket straight up to a second-floor window!

"See!" Hillary said with some satisfaction.

As the girls watched from inside the hedge, the man pushed the second-floor window wide open. He flung a leg over the sill. In seconds, he had pulled himself into the brick house! He waved down at the truck before disappearing inside.

The truck driver lowered the crane and drove down the driveway. He looked carefully up and down the street. Then he pulled out, turned the corner, and was gone!

"Even better!" Hillary said. "This way there's much less chance of anyone catching them! The guy inside the house can just climb out a back window when he's finished. They probably meet somewhere away from the house!" She turned to Kelly Ann. "I think it's time to call Sergeant Thomas!" The sergeant was the girls' special friend on the Windsor police force.

"But we're not sure. . . ." Kelly Ann began. "Maybe there's a good explanation for all this."

"Can you think of one?" Hillary asked impatiently.

"Okay, then. You stay here and keep an eye on the house. I'll go look for a phone."

"What if he leaves?"

"Follow him!"

44

Hillary pulled her bike out of the hedge. "I'll be back right away," she promised her friend, and she sped off as fast as she could pedal.

Except for the white trucks, the neighborhood looked deserted. Then Hillary spotted a car in the garage of a long, low house on the next block. Maybe the owner would let her use the phone. She had just reached out to open the front gate when a big Doberman bounded across the yard barking furiously.

"On second thought," Hillary said, backing away from the gate, "I'll phone from a booth on Main Street."

She and Kelly Ann had turned left off Main Street, then right, and then left again to get here, hadn't they? Or was it two rights and a left? Hillary shook her head. She was a little confused.

"Well, this is north Windsor," she said out loud, "so Main Street must be south of here." She looked at the sun, which was beginning to sink behind the trees. "If the sun is setting, that has to be west, and south ought to be this way," she decided.

It didn't quite work out that way, but finally Hillary spotted the city hall clock tower through the trees. City hall was at the end of Main Street. Soon she was in a phone booth, dialing the police emergency number.

"Hello!" she said when a woman's voice answered. "I want to report a burglary in progress in north Windsor!"

"What is the address?" the woman asked.

"The address!" Hillary smacked her forehead. She hadn't paid any attention to the street name! "I don't know," she said. "But if someone in a patrol car could meet me on Main Street, I could take him to the place. My name is Hillary Barnett—Sergeant Thomas knows me."

"Please hold on," the woman told her.

Hillary fidgeted in the phone booth until a man's voice came on the line. "Hillary, this is Officer Waters. What's this about a burglary?"

"Kelly Ann and I just saw a man break into a house in north Windsor," Hillary said. "He's working with a guy who drives one of those cable-TV trucks. They backed up under a second-floor window, and the driver lifted the burglar to it on a little crane. It's probably the same man who broke into the second floor of the Colwells' house and the apartments at Thornton Crescent. Kelly Ann's keeping an eye on him," she finished.

"Where are you?" Officer Waters asked quickly.

"On the corner of Main Street and Woodlawn," Hillary told him.

"We're on our way," said Officer Waters.

Kelly Ann watched Hillary until she turned the corner. Then she crept forward in the bushes so that she could look straight at the upstairs window, and she settled down to wait.

Hillary was more likely to rush into things than she was. But this time, she had to admit, her friend must be right. A person wouldn't climb into the upstairs window of a house like that unless he was up to something, as Hillary had said.

A blue jay screeched in a pine tree. Two squirrels fought over an acorn, unaware of the girl in the hedge. The second hand crawled around and around Kelly Ann's watch. Where was Hillary? She should have gotten back before now with the police. If she didn't hurry, the man would leave with his loot—and Kelly Ann would have to follow him! The idea was kind of scary. . . .

Kelly Ann looked at her watch again. The burglar had been inside for quite a while now. "He must be going through every room!" she said to herself. Then she remembered what Hillary had said about him climbing out a rear window. What if he'd already sneaked away from the back of the house? The police would come, and there would be no burglar!

Kelly Ann peered through the bushes at the house. There—wasn't that someone moving past a window on the *first* floor?!

She jumped to her feet. She had to move to another hiding place, so that she could see the burglar if he tried to slip out the back! Luckily, there were several clumps of bushy fir trees dotting the wide lawn. Keeping an eye on the downstairs window, Kelly Ann raced across the grass to the first clump. She bent down behind a juniper to catch her breath. Then she dashed over to a group of pines and kneeled down again. She could see the back of the house now, just as clearly as the side. The burglar definitely wouldn't be able to make a getaway without her knowing it.

Suddenly the back door rattled! Kelly Ann gasped. "Oh, no! He's coming out!" she whispered. "Hillary, where are you?"

The man in the blue shirt pushed open the screen door with his elbow and came out carrying a large plastic garbage can! Had he stolen so much stuff he needed something big to carry it in? He walked down the steps and headed across the backyard. Kelly Ann braced herself to follow him. She watched as he stopped next to a small shed. He opened the door and raised the garbage can up. . .TRASH! He was throwing out the *trash*!

The man strolled back to the house with the empty garbage can and shut the back door behind him.

Kelly Ann was so surprised that she stood up and took a step toward the house. "Burglars don't throw out trash!" she said. It looked as if she and Hillary had been wrong about the whole thing.

Suddenly several things happened at once. Officer Haney came running around the house with his hand on his gun! "Is he still in there?" he asked sharply.

"Yes, but—" Kelly Ann began.

"Get down behind those trees!" Officer Haney ordered. He moved quickly along the back wall of the house toward the door.

At the same time Kelly Ann could hear someone banging on the front door. "Open up!" It was Officer Waters. "Police!"

"Wait!" Kelly Ann yelled, running toward the front of the house. But she was too late. Officer Waters was already talking to the man in the blue shirt.

"Police!" the man was saying. "What's the problem?"

"That's him!" Hillary called from the patrol car at the end of the driveway. She paid no attention to Kelly Ann, who was shaking her head.

"We've had a report of a burglary at this address," Officer Waters said.

"That's impossible," replied the man in the blue shirt. "There's no one in the house but me."

"What is your name and address?" Officer Waters asked. He pulled a small notebook out of his pocket.

"John Franklin," the man answered. "I live

here."

"Why would you crawl through an upstairs window to get into your own house?" asked Officer Waters.

Mr. Franklin laughed. "I locked myself out," he explained. "I didn't want to break in through a downstairs window and set off the burglar alarm. I know how much you guys like false alarms," he said with a grin. "So I asked one of the cable people to boost me upstairs. Those windows aren't wired."

Officer Waters checked Mr. Franklin's driver's license to confirm his identity. Then he closed his notebook and slipped it back into his pocket. He glanced at Kelly Ann, who blushed a bright red. "I want to apologize for troubling you," Officer Waters told Mr. Franklin.

"Quite all right," Mr. Franklin said. "Makes me feel good to know someone is keeping a close eye on the neighborhood, with that cat burglar around."

Officer Waters called out to Officer Haney, and they walked back to the patrol car with a very embarrassed Kelly Ann bringing up the rear.

"He lives here," Officer Waters said to Hillary, who had climbed out of the car to meet them.

"But what about—" Hillary protested.

"He'd locked himself out, and the cable-TV

man helped him get back in," Kelly Ann told her.

"Oh," said Hillary. "Sorry," she added in a small voice.

"I know you girls are upset about M.C. getting that write-up in the paper and all," Officer Haney said. "And I'm sure it looked funny to see a guy climbing in an upstairs window."

"Sorry," Hillary said again.

"All in a day's work," said Officer Waters. "Don't worry—we'll find the real burglar." He lifted Hillary's bike out of the trunk of the car and set it on the ground. "We'll keep you posted," he promised. Then the patrol car rolled away, leaving the two girls feeling embarrassed and let down.

Kelly Ann dragged her own bike out of the hedge. "I think" she finally said, "that we do better when we wait for a clue from M.C."

"You're right," Hillary admitted. "But I wish he'd hurry up. We can't wait forever!"

Chapter Seven

Kelly Ann's mother answered Hillary's knock at the McCoys' the next afternoon. "Kelly Ann's upstairs in her room," she told Hillary. "Her Do Not Disturb sign is up. But I'm sure that doesn't apply to you."

Kelly Ann was lying on her stomach on her bed under the eaves. Spread out in front of her was a street map of Windsor.

"The map from the counterfeiting case!" Hillary said excitedly. "Do you have a plan?"

Kelly Ann shook her head. "Have you seen the new *Watchman*?" she asked gloomily.

Hillary's face fell. "*Now* what?"

"Another burglary," Kelly Ann said. "Same kind of thing, second-floor window. The burglar went through all the drawers in the bedroom and took money and jewelry. Even some costume jewelry was stolen."

"When did it happen?" Hillary asked.

"Yesterday afternoon, probably right about the time we had the police at the brick house."

"No clues?" asked Hillary, flopping down on the bed next to her friend.

"Not one," Kelly Ann replied. "But at least M.C. wasn't spotted at the scene of the crime."

"That's something. Where was the burglary?" Hillary asked, looking at the Windsor map.

Kelly Ann tapped a red X she'd drawn on the map. "Right here—Woodland Street, on the other side of the park."

She pointed to the other red Xs. "Here's the Colwells' house and Thornton Crescent Apartments. But as far as I can tell, there's really no pattern to the break-ins."

"Except that they're all pretty close to the park," said Hillary.

"That just makes good sense," Kelly Ann told her. "The park would be a great place for a burglar to hide."

Hillary sighed. "M.C. will just have to live up to his reputation and help us out," she said. "Is he around?"

"He hasn't shown up yet," Kelly Ann said.

"Some detective," said Hillary. "He's probably eating his way across town." The big gray cat had been known to stop for handouts at several houses between the Barnetts' and the McCoys'.

Suddenly the girls heard Andrew and Michael talking excitedly. Then there was a loud knock on Kelly Ann's door.

"Go away!" Kelly Ann said crossly. "Don't you see the sign?"

"There's an elephant coming down the street!" Andrew shouted through the door.

"And there's a walrus in the bathtub!" his sister said disgustedly. "You're as bad as Sara Darby."

Hillary raised herself off the bed and looked out the window. But Kelly Ann's bedroom faced the backyard, so she couldn't see anything.

"There really is!" Michael insisted.

"It's just a trick to get us to open the door," Kelly Ann assured Hillary. "They do this all the time."

The next thing they heard was the blast of a car horn. Samantha barked, and the McCoys' front door banged several times.

Kelly Ann went to the bedroom door. She opened it and looked into the hall. "They're gone," she announced, looking puzzled.

Hillary walked past her and up the hall to the twins' room. She pushed open their window and leaned out. "There *is* an elephant!" she exclaimed. "Come on!"

The girls raced down the stairs and out the front door. Next door, on the Johnsons' front lawn, stood a full-grown elephant! It ignored Samantha, who was barking frantically at its heels. It paid no attention to the people standing a short distance away. Instead, it snacked on Mrs. Johnson's flowers. As Kelly Ann and Hillary joined Mrs. McCoy and the twins, the ele-

phant stuffed a large petunia plant, roots and all, into its mouth with its trunk.

"I know that elephant," Andrew said firmly. "I'm going to talk to him."

"Oh, no, you don't!" his mother said, grabbing his arm and holding on to Michael's as well.

"It's Hector!" Andrew insisted.

"Are you sure? All elephants look pretty much alike," Michael said more cautiously.

Kelly Ann was becoming concerned about their dog. "Samantha is too old for so much excitement," she said. "I think we'd better call the circus."

"Or the police," said Mrs. McCoy. She pulled on the twins' arms. "Onto the front porch, everyone. Right now."

The twins were saved by the timely arrival of a small red truck. The passenger door swung open, and out hopped Al the elephant man!

"Hey, Al!" Andrew shouted.

"It's us!" Michael added.

"Hello, boys!" Al called back. "I'll be with you in just a minute."

He trotted past Samantha, right up to the elephant. "Patty, shame on you!" he scolded.

"It *isn't* Hector," Michael said to Andrew.

"This is the third time in four months you've run off!" Al went on. "People are going to think we don't feed you enough."

"She looks plenty fat to me," Andrew said to

Michael. Patty didn't stop chewing, but she did stretch out her trunk to stroke Al's face.

"That'll do!" Al said sternly. "I've already seen two fences you knocked down, and now you're ruining this garden." He hooked his arm around her trunk. "Fun's over. We're going home now."

Al and Patty moved steadily up the street, to stop in front of the McCoys and Hillary. "Please tell your neighbors to send a bill for their flowers to Mr. Baker at the circus," Al said to Mrs. McCoy. "He'll take care of it right away."

"I'll do that," Mrs. McCoy said. She grabbed Samantha's collar and dragged her up on the curb.

"Like to walk Patty back with me?" Al asked the twins.

"Can we, Mom?" Andrew begged.

"Well...if Kelly Ann and Hillary want to go with you," Mrs. McCoy answered.

"Sure!" Hillary spoke up, reaching out to touch Patty's wrinkled gray hide.

The children set off up the street with Al and Patty, a small parade of their own.

"Patty likes to get out sometimes, to see the sights," Al told them. "She's run off in Pittsburgh, Baltimore, even in Chicago. When we finally caught up with her in Chicago, she was taking a bath in Lake Michigan!"

The children laughed.

"I know you take care of the elephants," Michael said to Al. "But do you train them, too?"

"You bet I do!" Al answered. "When we get back, maybe you'd like to see a few of Patty's tricks."

The elephant lumbered through the park, startling a few bicycle riders and roller skaters. She pulled off bits of trees and bushes along the way and chewed contentedly. She didn't really seem to mind going back to the circus.

As they circled the main tent, old Hector raised his trunk and trumpeted cheerfully.

"See, Patty, your gang missed you," Al said to the elephant. Then he turned to the four children. "If you'll just sit on those bales of hay right there, I'll show you what the old girl can do."

He reached into the back of the nearest truck and pulled out a long, thin whip.

"You're not going to hit her, are you?" Michael asked with a frown.

"No way," Al assured him. "I use the whip as kind of a pointer. Patty!" he spoke firmly to the elephant. "Up!"

Patty watched him closely. When he raised the tip of the whip, she raised her front legs off the ground—higher, higher, until all of her great weight was balanced on her back legs!

"Good girl!" Al said. As he lowered the whip, Patty lowered herself back down onto all four legs.

Hillary, Kelly Ann, and the twins clapped loudly.

"This one is much harder," Al told them. "A headstand." He touched the top of the whip to the ground. "Patty, head!"

Patty's performance was interrupted by the great rattling roar of a lion.

"Uh-oh, Leroy!" Al said. "The last time he sounded like that, he had somebody hemmed into a corner." He dropped the whip and quickly fitted a steel ring around one of Patty's front legs. Then he ran toward the last of the huge circus trucks.

There was another rattling roar, ending in a throaty, coughing sound.

"A lion!" Kelly Ann said uneasily. "We'd better stay right here."

Then they heard someone shout, "There's a house cat in Leroy's cage!"

House cat? Hillary and Kelly Ann stared at each other. There was no reason to think it was M.C., but what house cat would get itself into that kind of trouble—*except* M.C.?

"Mystery Cat?" they said at the same time.

Chapter Eight

"Don't move off those hay bales—I mean it!" Kelly Ann said sharply to her little brothers. Then she and Hillary ran toward the last trailer truck.

On one side, steel panels had been slid back, exposing a row of animal cages. In the first cage some leopards paced back and forth. The next cage was empty. There were three lions in the third cage, all females. The noise was coming from the last cage.

A man brushed past the girls, calling to someone over his shoulder: "I'll get Sonny. He's working the tigers in the main tent!"

"There's Al!" Hillary said to Kelly Ann.

Al stood close to the fourth cage. He was holding one end of a long pole. The other end of the pole was inside the cage. Each time he moved his arms, there was a great rattling roar.

"You kids stay back!" a woman in black tights warned. "We don't want Leroy to get any more excited than he already is."

"Here!" Hillary pulled on Kelly Ann's arm. "If we climb onto the hood of this old car. . ."

The girls climbed up on the car and stared over everyone's heads into the fourth cage. A big, black-maned lion was lashing out at the pole Al held. His front paws were as big as dinner plates!

"I don't see a cat," Kelly Ann murmured. "What's Al trying to do, anyway?"

The girls were standing in bright sunlight, which made it hard to see inside the dark cage. But suddenly Hillary gasped. "It *is* M.C.!" She pointed to the right side of the cage. "Next to the wall near the back! Al's trying to keep the lion away from him."

Sure enough, against the side of the cage, mashing himself as flat as he could, was Mystery Cat!

"Oh, no!" Kelly Ann said. "Why did he go in there?"

Hillary groaned. "Why doesn't he squeeze out through the bars?"

"He's afraid to move," Kelly Ann answered.

Leroy growled again. It was a deep, rumbling sound the girls could feel in their chests. He tried to slap the pole aside, so he could slip around it to M.C.'s side of the cage.

"I can't watch!" Kelly Ann said in a strangled voice. She covered her eyes with her hands.

"Wait, it's okay. Al hit Leroy's nose with the pole! The lion's back on his side!" Hillary had to raise her voice to be heard over the roar that

61

followed.

Then a short man with slicked-back blond hair trotted up to the trailer truck. He carried a three-legged stool in one hand, a long whip in the other.

"Just in time, Sonny," Al said. "I'm getting kind of tired swinging this pole around."

Sonny nodded. "Sounds like Leroy's feeling pretty tough today," he said. "Just keep it up a minute longer, until I can get inside." He turned to the young man with him. "The cage is too small for me to use the whip at all," he said. "We'll just have to do it with the stool."

The two of them ducked around the back of the truck. Leroy took another swipe at the pole Al held. Suddenly a door slid up, low in the back wall of the cage. It was about three and a half feet high and two feet wide.

"Lion sized," Hillary observed.

Leroy whirled around to stare at the opening. Now Sonny's head and shoulders appeared as he bent down to get through the doorway. He stood up inside the lion's cage. "You can quit now, Al," Sonny said evenly.

Al pulled the pole out of the cage. He moved closer to the side where M.C. was huddled and stood ready to help.

Sonny began to talk to the lion in a soothing voice. Leroy grew quieter, but his eyes were fixed on the blond man. Deliberately, he took a step toward Sonny.

Sonny raised the stool. He held it out toward Leroy. Leroy gave a thunderous roar, but Sonny held the stool steady as a rock. Now Sonny took a step forward, toward the lion. Leroy grumbled and slapped at the stool. Sonny took another step forward. Leroy took a step backward. Slowly, slowly, Leroy began to back up.

"Whew!" Hillary sighed and Kelly Ann let out the breath she'd been holding, too.

One step at a time, the trainer backed the lion into a front corner of the cage, near the bars. "Come on in, Tom," he said softly.

His young assistant squeezed through the low door into the cage. Leroy's gaze shifted to the newcomer, but Sonny's low steady voice seemed to reassure him. His eyes returned to his trainer's face and he reached out again for the three-legged stool. Then he growled, baring huge, yellow fangs.

"Did you see that?" Hillary exclaimed.

Kelly Ann was watching the young man named Tom. Cautiously he skirted the edge of the cage, moving toward M.C. but never taking his eyes off Leroy. Carefully he reached down for the gray cat. He picked him up, then pressed him against his shirt. Then he slowly retreated the way he had come.

Leroy glanced in Tom's direction, but he seemed more interested in what Sonny was saying. Tom crouched and slipped out of the cage through the small door. Then Sonny backed safely out of the cage, too.

The group of motionless onlookers stirred to life.

"Good work, Sonny," Al said, stepping forward to tap him on the shoulder.

"Looks like a stray," said Tom, still holding M.C., who wasn't moving at all.

"I don't think so," Al began.

"He's ours!" Hillary broke in. She and Kelly Ann jumped down from the car and hurried over to collect a badly shaken Mystery Cat.

"How in the world did the cat get in there in the first place?" the woman in black tights was saying. "That's what I don't understand. The space between the bars is so narrow. I don't see how he possibly could have jumped between them. It just doesn't make sense."

Tenderly, Kelly Ann took M.C. from Tom and held him close. He was still stiff with fear, and she could feel his heart beating wildly against her hands. "It's okay now," she whispered, her mouth against his notched ear.

Hillary rubbed M.C.'s back. "How *could* he have gotten inside—not to mention why would he have *wanted* to!"

"What's all the noise?" a new voice drawled. It was Zack Jennings, lounging against a parked car with his arms crossed.

"Cat was in Leroy's cage," Tom said shortly, pointing to M.C.

"Oh, yeah?" Zack's gaze swept across the cat and lingered on the girls' faces. "Good thing you got him out or he would've been lion dinner." He grinned unpleasantly. "And he looks so tough and stringy, he would have made Leroy sick."

"Hey, listen!" Hillary said, furious.

Kelly Ann grabbed her friend's arm and pulled her away. She had just noticed three deep scratches running along the underside of Zack's right arm—scratches that looked strangely familiar!

Chapter Nine

"But—" Hillary protested.

"Come on!" Kelly Ann urged her friend.

"He's a big bully!" Hillary huffed as she followed Kelly Ann. They were headed in the direction of the elephant truck.

Kelly Ann stopped walking as soon as they were out of earshot. "Didn't you see Zack's arm?" she asked in a low voice.

"No," Hillary answered. "What about it?"

"Three long, thin scratches, still bleeding," said Kelly Ann. "I'm pretty sure they were M.C.'s! I got some exactly like them the last time I gave him a flea bath."

"You mean *Zack* put M.C. into Leroy's cage?" Hillary asked.

"I think so," Kelly Ann said grimly.

"Why?" Hillary demanded. "Unless—Let's think for a minute." She frowned with concentration. "What if Zack had something to do with the burglaries, and M.C. was on his trail?"

"Zack?" said Kelly Ann. "How could he get up to those second-floor windows in Thornton Crescent or at the Colwells'? Fly?"

"I guess you're right," Hillary muttered.

"Hold it!" Kelly Ann said suddenly. "Zack couldn't do it, but what about Pico?"

"The monkey!" Hillary exclaimed. "Remember when Sara said she saw a monkey? You thought it was only a squirrel. But what if it really *was* a monkey—Pico!"

M.C. had started to wriggle impatiently in Kelly Ann's arms. She scratched the cat behind the ears, and then she went on. "You know how angry M.C. got when the monkey pulled his tail? He never forgets stuff like that. Maybe he was trying to catch the monkey at the Colwells'. He followed Pico up the tree, then he got stuck. Pico stole the purse and the jewelry, and M.C. got blamed!"

"But Zack's the real bad guy," Hillary said. "I'll bet he trained Pico to steal! M.C., you've done it again! We've got our man, and you gave us the clues to prove it."

"Wait a minute," Kelly Ann said. "Maybe not. The burglaries at Thornton Crescent took place while the circus was going on—the little boy told us so. The same at the Colwells'. Sara and I heard the circus band playing before the police drove up."

"Maybe Zack's not in every show," suggested Hillary. "Or maybe he's just in at the beginning or the end. That would give him time to pull off the burglaries without anyone missing him."

"That might work," Kelly Ann said.

"I know—let's ask Al!" said Hillary.

"Okay, but don't say anything about the burglaries yet," Kelly Ann warned. "We really don't have any proof, and remember what happened the last time we accused someone!"

"Don't remind me," Hillary said, rolling her eyes. Then the two girls hurried off to find Al and ask him their question.

"Zack's in the show right at the beginning," the elephant man told them. "Everybody has to be in the spec—that's short for 'spectacle,' the parade at the start of every performance. Then ...let me see...about a third of the way through, he's on again. He's in a routine with a few of the other clowns, between the Spanish web and me and the baby elephants."

"Zack's a clown?" Hillary couldn't believe it.

"Yep. White face, orange wig, painted smile, baggy suit—the whole thing," Al said. "Then he and the monkey do a routine after the pony act and before the leopards. That's it. Except he always hangs around in the alley watching the whole show. He gets in the way and generally makes a nuisance of himself."

According to what Al had said, Zack had no opportunity to leave the circus and come back late in the show. The girls tried to hide their disappointment.

"Why do you want to know?" Al asked.

69

"Oh, we just wondered what he does," Hillary answered, trying to sound casual.

"Al, thank you so much for keeping Leroy away from M.C.," Kelly Ann said, quickly changing the subject. "You saved our cat's life!"

"I thought he was a goner for sure," Al admitted. "Cat almost used up all nine of his lives at once."

"We'd better go home," Kelly Ann said to her little brothers.

"Bye, Al," Andrew said.

"See you Thursday," said Michael.

"Why Thursday?" Kelly Ann asked.

"Dad's taking us all to the circus on Thursday night," Michael told her.

"Isn't that great?" said Andrew.

"Then you'll see Patty do all of her tricks," Al said, "without any interruptions from Leroy."

The children waved good-bye and started back across the park.

"Here—I'll hold him for a while." Hillary took M.C. Then as the twins rushed ahead, she added, "I guess it can't be Zack, after all."

Kelly Ann sighed. "I guess not. But I'm still going to keep an eye on him Thursday evening."

"If only you could talk," Hillary said to M.C., giving him a big squeeze.

"MROOW!" the cat snarled.

"It's probably just as well we didn't understand *that*," Hillary said with a grin.

Chapter Ten

Thursday afternoon, Kelly Ann and the twins raced through their homework the minute they got home from school. Mr. McCoy finished a roofing job early to be ready for dinner by five-thirty. And at twenty to seven, everybody except Kelly Ann piled into Mrs. McCoy's old car. It coughed and stalled twice before it backed slowly out of the garage.

Kelly Ann removed M.C.—and his dinner—from the back porch and carried them into the garage. Hurriedly she slid the door closed. "I know you don't like this," she apologized to the cat through the crack, "but at least I won't have to worry about where you are. I'll let you out when we get back," she promised. She then jumped into the car with the rest of the family.

"We're going to the circus!" Michael bounced up and down on the backseat.

"From what I hear, you're at the circus most of the time," Mr. McCoy teased.

"It's not the same thing," Andrew answered quickly.

It certainly wasn't! The midway leading to

the main tent blazed with lights. Crowds of people wove back and forth, visiting the smaller tents and buying things to eat and drink.

"Can we have some cotton candy?" Andrew asked his father.

"Why not?" said Mr. McCoy.

"We'll have to go inside and sit down before you eat it," Mrs. McCoy told the twins. "Otherwise you'll get it all over your clothes."

"And in our hair," Michael added with a grin, remembering what had happened at the carnival last year.

Mr. McCoy handed a bill to the man behind the counter at one of the stands. "Two cotton candies, please," he said. "Kelly Ann—what about you? Eileen?" he asked his wife.

Kelly Ann and her mother chose candied apples. Then they all watched as the man rolled first one cardboard cone and then another around and around the cotton candy machine. He handed the cones piled high with sugary pink fluff to the boys.

The family followed Mr. McCoy to the booth outside the main tent, where he bought their tickets.

"Okay—straight ahead," Mrs. McCoy directed the twins.

The tent looked even larger inside. There were big rings for the performers and a ceiling stretching way up the center pole.

"Where do you want to sit?" Mr. McCoy asked.

"Here!" Andrew shouted.

"There!" said Michael.

"Let's sit closer to that end, so we can watch the circus people walk in and out," Kelly Ann suggested.

"Okay," the twins agreed.

"That way we can see Al when he comes in," Michael said.

"And Patty and Hector," added his twin.

"And Zack Jennings," Kelly Ann said to herself.

The McCoys climbed up into the bleachers and sat down. More and more people poured into the tent. The members of the circus band tuned up their instruments. The house lights dimmed.

"It's starting!" Andrew said, his mouth and chin sticky with cotton candy.

"Steady," warned Mr. McCoy, as Michael waved his cone around wildly.

The band hit a high note and held it. A spotlight lit up the performers' entrance to the big tent.

"Al!" squealed Michael, as an elephant came through the canvas doorway in time to the music. Al walked by its side in a red suit with shiny trim.

"That's Hector!" Andrew said importantly.

73

"You thought *Patty* was Hector," Michael pointed out.

"Sssh!" said their mother. "Look at the beautiful horses!"

The house lights brightened, and three golden palominos pranced into the tent. A young woman in a purple tutu waved to the audience as she stood on the back of the middle horse. Then came the jugglers, the tumblers, and the poodles the children had seen on their first visit to the circus backyard. The big white dogs walked into the tent on their hind legs. The biggest dog turned slowly around as it walked.

"Here come the clowns!" announced Mr. McCoy.

There were short clowns wearing enormous shoes and tiny hats. There were sad clowns and clowns with happy faces. There was even a clown on stilts whose legs looked ten feet long.

Kelly Ann searched the crowd of clowns for Zack. Would she be able to recognize him? As it turned out, it wasn't at all difficult to pick him out. Pico sat on his shoulder, wearing a little green cap.

Zack himself was dressed in a baggy suit of big black-and-white checks. His black hair was completely covered by a frizzy orange wig. A huge smile never left his chalk-white face. It was painted on in red and black, and he had a large red false nose. In one of his white-gloved hands,

he held the end of Pico's short leash.

"The baby elephants!" said Andrew.

"The leopard we saw the other day!" said Michael.

But the rest of the circus parade was lost on Kelly Ann. She kept her eyes fixed on Zack and the monkey as they circled the three rings. She watched them until they had walked back through the canvas doorway and the "spec" was over. She wasn't sure what she expected to see, but if Zack made even one false move she didn't want to miss it.

The house lights dimmed again. The band played a lively tune while men in overalls put together a large cage in the middle ring. Then the ringmaster announced the first act: "The greatest lion tamer in the world—Sonny Harkin!"

M.C.'s rescuer was dressed in a shining silver jumpsuit. His slicked-back hair gleamed as he bowed to the crowd.

"Is that the man who got M.C. out of the lion's cage?" Mr. McCoy asked Kelly Ann.

Kelly Ann nodded. She'd told her parents about M.C.'s misadventure. But she hadn't told them about Zack Jennings's scratches.

Suddenly four lions and two tigers came bounding down a chute leading to the big cage. A door clanged shut behind them. The animals paced back and forth, glaring at the audience. Black-maned Leroy roared loudly and swatted at the lion next to him. Then all of the big cats hissed and snarled.

"Wow!" Michael said in awe. "Leroy's mean!"

Sonny Harkin didn't appear to be frightened by the animals' bad tempers. When he stepped into the cage with his whip, each of the cats jumped onto a tiny platform. Soon Sonny had them sitting up on their hind legs, leaping over his whip. The tigers even balanced on large wooden balls.

"He's good!" said Mr. McCoy.

At the end of the act, the houselights dimmed. Sonny took a match and lit the edges of a huge hoop. One by one, the cats jumped through the flaming ring. Then he took his bows to loud applause. Leroy—with a last angry growl at the crowd—led the other cats back up the chute and out of the main tent.

While the cage was being taken apart, the spotlight shone on the Bianco family. They performed on a trampoline in the ring closest to the McCoys.

"Two parents and three kids, just like us," Michael said.

"What if we did that?" Andrew suggested. He pointed to the smallest boy, who looked as if he were about the twins' age. "He probably doesn't even have to go to school!"

"The Magnificent Flying McCoys!" announced Mr. McCoy. He and his wife laughed.

Even Kelly Ann giggled at the thought of her family doing double backflips on a trampoline.

"It's a lot of work. Besides, I'm sure the children have to study every day," Mrs. McCoy told the twins. "They probably have a correspondence course they follow until the circus stops traveling for the winter."

Next was the Spanish web, with two women twirling on ropes high above the audience. Then on came the clowns, just as Al had told the children they would. Zack was easy to spot in his black-and-white suit. He was riding on the back of a tiny fire truck. He raced around the center ring on the way to an imaginary fire. Pico wore a fireman's hat.

The twins clapped loudly as the group roared out of the tent. They clapped even louder when they saw the next act trot in: Al's baby elephants. Each one used his trunk to hold on to the tail of the elephant in front of him. The lead baby held on to Al's hand.

They sat up as the children had seen Patty do. They stood on their hind legs and rested their front legs on one another's backs. Finally, they lay down and pretended to sleep. Kelly Ann saw little of their routine, however. She had noticed the black-and-white clown suit near the performers' entrance. Zack Jennings stood there with Pico on his shoulder, apparently watching the show. He stayed to watch the jugglers, the magician who sawed a lady in half, the tumblers, and the high-wire act.

"Al was right—Zack never leaves the tent, and neither does Pico," Kelly Ann said to herself. "But if he wasn't involved in the burglaries, why would he have shoved M.C. into Leroy's cage?"

After the ponies left the ring, Zack and Pico were on again. They played baseball with an invisible ball. Pico hit a home run. They juggled small colored rings. Pico even rode a unicycle. After they had taken their bows, they walked over to the bleachers where the McCoys were sitting to say hello to some of the children.

"I want to shake hands with the monkey!" Andrew shouted.

"Me, too!" said Michael.

The twins stretched forward as the clown in the black-and-white suit leaned toward them. Suddenly, Kelly Ann spotted something strange. At the base of the clown's neck, between his frizzy orange wig and his collar, was one long blond curl. Zack Jennings had short *black* hair!

Chapter Eleven

"Absolutely not!" Mrs. McCoy said firmly as she pulled into the driveway later that night. "It's much too late to call the Barnetts'. You can tell Hillary about the circus tomorrow."

Kelly Ann sighed as she got out of the car. She couldn't explain the real reason why she wanted to call her best friend, so she let the subject drop. Then she had an idea: Maybe she could get M.C. to carry a message for her! She slid the garage door open slowly. The big gray cat streaked out into the night without a backward glance. He was on his way to Hillary's, no doubt, but without her message. She sighed again. There was no getting around it; her news would have to wait until morning.

At first light the next day, Kelly Ann crept downstairs to the phone in the hall. Making hardly a sound, she dialed Hillary's private number.

Hillary grabbed the phone on the first ring. "I was just about to call you!" she said. "Did anything happen last night?"

Quickly, Kelly Ann told her about seeing the

long blond curl beneath the frizzy orange wig.

"Of course!" said Hillary. "Zack and the blond lady are about the same size. She dresses up in his clown suit, paints her face, and everybody thinks it's Zack. Meanwhile Zack can go out and do the burglaries during the show. He always has the perfect alibi! He was at the circus the whole time!"

"Right," said Kelly Ann.

"There's just one thing, though," Hillary said. "If the monkey stays with the blond woman through the whole show, who is climbing up to those second-story windows?"

"Oh, I didn't think of that," Kelly Ann said, sounding discouraged.

"Never mind," Hillary said. "I still think Zack's the one behind all this. If my plan works, tomorrow we'll find out how he does it."

"What plan?" Kelly Ann asked.

"Well, my grandmother Margaret is coming to visit for the weekend," Hillary told her. "She loves the circus, and she wants to take me to the Saturday afternoon show. So while I work the inside, you can work the outside."

"What do you mean, 'work the outside'?" Kelly Ann asked.

"I mean, you can ride over on your bike, hide near the elephants' truck or something, and keep an eye on Zack's camper."

"I don't know. . ." Kelly Ann said hesitantly.

"Didn't Zack stuff M.C. into Leroy's cage?" Hillary demanded. "We have to catch that guy!"

That reminder convinced Kelly Ann. "You're right!" she said. "Let's just hope Zack *does* try something. Tomorrow's the last day the circus will be in Windsor."

"Kelly Ann, aren't you getting ready for school?" Mrs. McCoy called from the top of the stairs.

"Right, Mom," Kelly Ann replied. "Have to go," she said to Hillary.

"That's okay. We'll work out the details later," Hillary promised, and then both girls hung up.

As they had suspected, a burglary *had* been committed on Thursday night. The *Windsor Watchman* reported that a house had been robbed sometime between eight and ten o'clock, while the family was out at the movies. "And while the circus was going on," Kelly Ann thought when she read the story. "Thank goodness M.C. was safe in the garage!"

Early Saturday afternoon found Kelly Ann hiding behind two huge wheels, keeping an eye on Zack's brown camper. She was crouched under the empty sleeper truck, trying to stay out of sight until the circus began. To her right, Al was buckling a red-and-gold harness on Hector. She could hear him talking quietly to the elephant. To her left, a woman was helping her daughter fasten the neck of her costume. Nearby three young men were laughing as they juggled cups and bowls and plates. Then the circus band started tuning up, and all the performers began to move toward the main tent. It was almost time for the spec, the parade that started the show.

The door to Zack's camper opened. A clown in a black-and-white-checked suit appeared, a monkey sitting on his shoulder. At the bottom of the steps the clown paused to adjust his frizzy orange wig. The narrow door of the camper slowly closed by itself!

"Somebody's in there, all right!" Kelly Ann murmured. "And if I'm not mistaken, it's a *he*, and that clown is a *she*!"

The clown joined the crowd of performers forming a long line just outside the back entrance. Inside, the circus band hit a high note and held it. Then it swung into the opening bars of a marching tune and the line of performers snaked forward, into the big tent.

Kelly Ann continued to watch the camper. She thought she saw the doorknob shake a little. Then slowly, the door opened again, and someone leaned out very cautiously. It was Zack Jennings!

Satisfied that he was alone, Zack jumped out of the camper and dashed behind it. But not before Kelly Ann saw what was poking out of the backpack he was wearing: the small, dark

83

head of a monkey!

The clown had carried a monkey on her shoulder. Zack had another monkey in his backpack. There were *two* of them!

"So that's how he does it!" Kelly Ann muttered. "He must always keep one of the monkeys hidden in the camper, so everybody thinks there's just one!"

Zack was rolling a bicycle toward the edge of the vacant lot. Kelly Ann crawled out from under the truck and got ready to follow him.

Hillary and her grandmother Margaret were comfortably seated when the spec began. Hillary saw Al and Hector, the palominos, the jugglers, and the tumblers. But the longer she sat, the more fidgety she became. The way she figured it, Zack Jennings would leave his camper during the parade, when every other performer was in the main tent.

She waited until the clown walked in and she had seen the black-and-white-suited clown carrying the monkey. Then she couldn't stand it any longer. "Margaret," she said, "I'll be right back. I'm dying for a candied apple."

"All right," her grandmother said. "But hurry, or you'll miss the first act."

Hillary jumped down from the bleachers and rushed for the door. Then she tore around the main tent.

The backyard looked deserted. The door on Zack's camper was ajar. Where could Kelly Ann be? Hillary's eyes fell on the bushes at the edge of the vacant lot. If Zack wanted to stay out of sight, he'd have headed in that direction, she reasoned.

She ran past the big trucks and into the brush. She almost tumbled over Kelly Ann, who was pumping up the front tire of her bicycle.

"Hillary!" Kelly Ann squeaked. "You scared me to death! My tire's flat."

"Where's Zack?" her friend asked.

"He's on the bike path, headed back that way." Kelly Ann motioned with her head back across the park.

"Enough air in the tire," Hillary said quickly. "Let's go!" She pulled Kelly Ann's bike down to the path and climbed on. "I'll pedal—I'm stronger."

Kelly Ann balanced on the crossbar, her legs dangling to one side. "What about your grandmother?" she asked.

"I hope she's so interested in the circus that she doesn't notice how long I'm gone," answered Hillary. She was pedaling for all she was worth.

"There's Zack, on the next hill!" Kelly Ann said. "See his green backpack?"

"Yeah," said Hillary. She was starting to puff a little.

"The monkey's in there," Kelly Ann said.

"The monkey was in the parade—I saw him!" Hillary declared.

"There are *two* of them," Kelly Ann told her. "I figure Zack keeps one of them hidden in the camper."

"Wow!" said Hillary. "Smart! I never would have thought of that!"

"Faster, he's speeding up!" Kelly Ann urged.

"I'm trying!" Hillary was breathing hard now.

Zack had reached the edge of the park. He turned left onto a paved street.

"He's headed toward my neighborhood!" said Kelly Ann.

Chapter Twelve

By the time the girls reached the paved road, Zack Jennings was nowhere to be seen. They turned left as Zack had done. But at the first intersection Hillary stopped the bike. "Now where?" she asked.

Kelly Ann slid down from the crossbar. Should they go straight? Or should they turn right, away from the park? She stared hopefully up the street, looking for a clue.

"We'd better make up our minds, fast!" Hillary said, surveying the neighborhood. "Hey, look at that cat! Doesn't that look like—"

"M.C.!" exclaimed Kelly Ann.

A large gray cat was crouched on the sidewalk near the other end of the block. It seemed to be staring at something across the street.

"Maybe he's spotted the monkey!" Kelly Ann said. "Let's get closer and see." She started to sit down on the crossbar of the bicycle, but Hillary stopped her.

"The tire's gone flat again!" Hillary said.

She pushed the bike up on the lawn of the nearest house. "We'll come back for it later."

"M.C.'s starting to creep forward," Kelly Ann told her.

"Then come on!" said Hillary.

"But stay off the sidewalk—stick to the yards! We don't want Zack to spot *us*."

The girls rode across lawns and squeezed through hedges. "There goes M.C.!" said Kelly Ann. She watched the cat leap across the street and into the yard of a big two-story house.

"Hurry!" urged Hillary.

They found M.C. staring up at a second-floor window, his tail lashing back and forth. The window was open just a crack. Along the side of the house a large wisteria vine climbed all the way to the roof.

"Couldn't be better for a monkey," Kelly Ann murmured.

"It looks as if the people who live there are out, and from the way M.C.'s acting, the monkey's already inside," Hillary said. "It's just like the other burglaries. But where is Zack?"

"He must keep out of sight and wait for the monkey to bring him the loot," suggested Kelly Ann.

"I'm going to go look for him. You try to grab the monkey when it climbs down," Hillary told her.

The garage was empty. Hillary walked around the house to the back. Cautiously, she pulled open the door to a small shed. But aside from several garbage cans, that was empty, too. She pushed through a row of scratchy ever-greens to see what lay beyond them.

Zack had stopped his bike in the shade of a tree, near the curb on the street behind. He was checking his watch when Hillary saw him.

"How am I supposed to grab the monkey?" Kelly Ann thought, straining her ears to catch any sounds coming from inside the house. She couldn't hear anything. But when M.C.'s ears pricked up, she was prepared to trust his judg-ment. Seconds later, a small, round head ap-peared over the windowsill.

The monkey eased out of the window and started climbing down the wisteria vine. As soon as he saw Kelly Ann, he changed course. Holding on to the vine with one hand, he swung way out. Then he silently dropped to the ground just out of her reach!

"Now I'll never catch him!" Kelly Ann mut-tered, sprinting after the monkey.

She'd forgotten about M.C.

"Rrorrw!" the gray cat snarled. He sprang at the monkey like a tiger! The monkey shrieked in alarm. He sped toward a tree at the back of the yard, with M.C. gaining on him with every step. Kelly Ann was close behind.

The monkey must have decided the tree was too far away, because he dodged suddenly...

into the doorway of the small shed. M.C. was right behind him, and with a bound, Kelly Ann slammed the door on them *both*!

On the other side of the block, Hillary was busy, too. Zack had climbed on his bike and pedaled it quickly to the end of the street. Hillary had run down the sidewalk after him. But he went so fast, she couldn't keep up. By the time she reached the corner, Zack was at the end of the next block. "He's circling around to pick up the monkey!" she decided.

A car horn sounded behind her. She ignored it and ran faster. The car honked again and again. Hillary peered over her shoulder. *Glynis!*

Her mother stopped her car and rolled down the window. "I'm sure you have a very good reason for why you aren't at the circus with your grandmother," she said grimly. "Perhaps you'd care to share it with me."

Mrs. Barnett drove the girls to the police station to make the report. Hillary had insisted that someone stay behind to guard the monkey, but Mrs. Barnett wouldn't hear of either girl staying there alone.

In the end it was Kelly Ann who thought of a solution to the problem. She found three large rocks at the edge of the yard. With Hillary's help, she carried them over to the garbage shed and piled them in front of the door.

"That should keep them in there for a while," Kelly Ann said with satisfaction. Then they all set off for the station.

"Please hurry," Hillary told her mother. "I'd like to get the monkey out of that shed while there's still some of him left."

"Where do you think Zack went?" Kelly Ann asked.

"He must have seen you standing in the yard and headed straight back to the circus," Hillary answered. "I bet he'll pretend he was there all the time, being a clown."

"That might have worked," Kelly Ann said, patting her pocket with a satisfied smile, "if we didn't have the monkey."

Half an hour later, a patrol car pulled into the circus backyard. Mrs. Barnett, Kelly Ann, and Hillary—carrying M.C.—climbed out of the backseat. Officers Haney and Waters got out of the front.

"Zack Jennings?" Officer Haney said, approaching the man in the black-and-white clown suit. "We'd like to ask you some questions about a burglary this afternoon."

"Burglary?" Zack said innocently. "What would I know about it? I was in the show all afternoon. Ask anybody."

Several of the other performers agreed.

"We have reason to believe it was someone

else who was in the show, disguised as you," said Officer Waters.

"Can you prove it?" Zack asked with a sly smile.

"There was also a monkey involved in the crime," Officer Haney went on.

"Well, Pico has been right here on my shoulder since the spec," Zack told him.

Officer Waters reached into the front seat of the patrol car and pulled out a large cardboard carton. "Not *that* monkey," he said. He opened the top of the box.

"Well, I'll be!" said Al the elephant man. "There are *two* of them, as alike as peas in a pod."

"With one difference," Officer Haney said. "This one is a professional burglar." He pointed to a small pouch strapped to the monkey's chest. "That bag's full of stolen jewelry."

When Hillary sat down to breakfast on Monday morning, her father handed her the newspaper. "There's something on page one that might interest you," he said.

At the top of the front page was an article about the burglaries. On the left was a photograph of M.C., on the right a picture of the monkey. The caption underneath read, "Cat Puts an End to Monkey Business."

M.C. definitely hadn't lost his touch.